Elijah and the Elephant

BY

SHEILA RIEDL

ISBN:

Softcover 978-1-4653-5796-0

To order additional copies of this book, contact:
Xlibris Corporation
1-888-795-4274
www.Xlibris.com
Orders@Xlibris.com

Dedicated to my kids who encouraged me every step of the way: Allison & Dustin Riedl

CHAPTER 1:
MEETING A NEW FRIEND

Elijah and her three friends are playing in the run down playground. It is full of tall grass. The fence is broken and the equipment is rusty. The girls don't mind. It is the only place they have to play outside. Today is the first day of school break.

Elijah is 10 years old. After her Dad died, her Mom had to start working a lot of hours to pay the bills. Since her Mom is always working, she never notices what Elijah is up to. They live in the poor part of a city in Africa. She is very friendly. She does what she wants and doesn't care what others think about her.

The four friends are very close. Elijah is always ready for an adventure, but she forgets about safety. Her friends are always trying to keep her safe. They try to keep her from her adventures. They usually end up joining her and having fun. They live in the same poor neighborhood.

Elijah heard an unusual noise behind her as she started up the ladder of the slide. She turned around to see what it was. She could see what appeared to be a gray animal sleeping on the other side of the broken fence. As she walked toward the fence she said, "What are you little fellow?" Just then, the sleeping animal awoke. It jumped up and made a loud trumpet noise! Elijah, startled, yelled and fell backward.

Her three friends stopped playing and stared in disbelief. They had all seen an elephant before. After all, they did live in Africa. However, they had never seen one in the city. Even though the elephant was small, the three friends were frozen with fear.

Elijah, being her normal adventurous self, stood up and walked toward the elephant. Her friends tried to stop her. Elijah ignored their warning as usual. She moved closer. She told her friends, "She looks scared. She is so young." As she approached, the elephant lowered her trunk. She seemed to be holding it out to shake her hand. Elijah said, "See. She is friendly. She wants to shake my hand."

Standing on her tip toes, Jasmine said, "I wonder where her Mom and Dad are." She had a concerned look on her face as she looked around.

Tera said, "I bet she is lost from her herd. This is the time of year they move."

Kendall said, "We have to tell someone. They can capture her and take her back to the wild."

"NO!", Elijah said firmly. "They will be mean to her. They will shoot her with a tranquilizer gun, throw her in a truck, and dump her." As she continued to pet the elephant, she asked her friends, "Can't you see she is friendly? Come pet her."

Still standing, Kendall repeated, "Elijah, we have to call someone." The other two friends moved cautiously toward the elephant. Reluctantly, Kendall finally joined them. The elephant greeted each of them with her trunk. The adventure had begun.

CHAPTER 2:
FINDING A PLACE

The girls started to discuss where they could keep her safe. They made plans on how they would each sneak food from their homes. They talked about how they could take care of her. They talked until it was time for lunch. They decided one of them should go home and bring back lunch for all of them. The other three would stay to keep an eye on the Elephant.

It was decided Tera would get lunch. The three friends were discussing a name for the Elephant when Tera returned. Elijah suddenly said, "Elle. You know, short for elephant." They all agreed this was this best name for their new friend. As the friends ate, they shared their apples and oranges with Elle. Elijah thought, What a great summer this is going to be.

After lunch, it was time to decide on a place to keep Elle. It is not easy to hide an elephant, even a small one. Elijah wanted the elephant to stay in her back yard. The others agreed. If anyone could hide an elephant in the city, it would be Elijah. Besides, they didn't want to get in trouble if someone discovered her at their house.

With that decided, they walked to Elijah's house. Elle followed them. She seemed to like her new friends as much as they liked her. She really liked the apples they gave her to eat. In Elijah's back yard, is a worn out shed. It looks like it could fall over if the wind blew hard enough. There was just enough room between the shed and the back fence to make a resting place for Elle. The bushes beside the fence would help hide her.

Elijah found the tub her Mom used to wash their clothes in. She washed it out and filled it with water. Elle drank the water quickly. Elijah had to fill it up again. While Elijah worked on the water supply, the other three friends went back to the playground. They each came back with their arms full of grass. They had to make several trips to have enough to make Elle a bed.

The friends were exhausted. They sat down and watched Elle rearrange her bed several times. Elle was finally satisfied and laid down for a nap. The girls sat for a while and watched Elle. They were excited about their new friend.

One by one, the friends had to go home. Elijah remained. She did not realize how fast the time was going. It was almost dark. Her Mom would be home soon. She knew she could not stay in the back yard. Her Mom would surely find Elle if she stayed. So, Elijah went into the house to get some food for Elle. She brought out the food, set it beside her, and told her goodnight.

As Elijah lay in bed that night, she was too excited to sleep. She started thinking about all of the adventures they would have. She hoped her new friend would stay.

CHAPTER 3:
THE NEXT DAY

As soon as her Mom was walking out the front door, Elijah headed out the back. She was anxious to see if Elle was there. Her heart beat faster as she walked closer to the shed. Elle startled Elijah when she greeted her with a loud trumpet hello. Elijah laughed at herself. She was happy to see Elle still there. She had eaten all the food and spilled the water tub.

Elijah was petting and talking to Elle when her friends arrived. They were happy to see she had stayed. Jasmine questioned Elijah about whether her Mom was suspicious. Elijah said, "She didn't even look out the back window."

The girls decided to take Elle back to the playground. They could play while she ate grass. Jasmine worried someone would see them. Tera assured her the adults were all at work. Besides, they were so busy they wouldn't even notice something as unusual as an elephant walking down the street. Kendall suggested they walk down the alley instead of the street. They all agreed.

The girls played until lunch time. Elle laid down for a nap. This time it was decided Jasmine would get lunch for the group. She looked concerned when she returned. Elijah asked, "What is wrong? Did someone see you?" Jasmine answered, "No, I am worried my Dad will be suspicious. I never eat fruit. Today I emptied the pantry." They broke into laughter as they watched their chubby friend plop on the ground.

After lunch, the friends took Elle for a walk in the field behind the playground. They showed her the way to their special place by the river. They watched Elle play in the water as she sprayed water everywhere. Elijah was the first one to join her in river. The others soon followed her. Elle enjoyed spraying her new friends.

The girls were tired. They lay on the river bank so their clothes could dry. Elle continued to play in the river. It was a hot day and the water felt good. Elle finally tired. She climbed on the river bank and lay down next to Elijah. She slept as the girls talked. They tried to think of things they could do with their new elephant friend.

When Elle awoke from her nap, the girls decided it was time to return to the city. They wanted to get Elle hidden before the adults started coming home from work. Elle seemed content to do whatever her friends were doing.

Elijah worked on settling Elle into her bed. The others went home to get her some food to eat during the night. Elle was feeling playful. When Elijah filled up the water tub, she put her foot on the edge and dumped it out. She trumpted at Elijah, as if to say, "Ha! Ha!" Elijah told her it wasn't funny. Elle seemed to understand. She didn't dump it the next time. By then, the other girls had returned. Elle seemed pleased with the dinner they brought her.

The girls each told her goodnight and left. It was harder for Elijah to leave her friend alone. Elle looked sad. She knew she had to go in the house before her Mom came home.

Elijah was finishing her chores when her Mom arrived home. Her Mom asked her how was her day. Elijah wanted to tell her all about Elle. She knew that her Mom wouldn't understand. Especially now, she was working so hard. She told her Mom what she could about her day.

That night, as she lay in bed, she thought about her Mom. She wished she didn't have to work so much. Her Mom was always so tired. She missed the fun things they would do together. She drifted off to sleep as she was trying to think of ways she could help her Mom.

CHAPTER 4:
SUMMER DAYS

The next few weeks were much the same. The girls would play in the playground in the morning. They took turns getting lunch. They played at the river in the afternoon. It was turning out to be a great summer. They hoped it would never end.

One night, as Elijah and her Mom ate supper, her Mom asked her what she had been doing all week. Elijah didn't want to lie to her Mom. She hoped one day soon she could tell her Mom all about Elle. She told her Mom about playing at the playground and at the river. Her Mom warned her to be careful at the river. She said, " You never know when a wild animal might show up for a drink." Elijah just smiled and shook her head.

After supper, Elijah's Mom checked the food pantry. She was making a grocery list. "I know we had more apples and oranges in here." she thought aloud. Elijah quickly excused herself to get ready for bed.

The next day Elijah told her friends about the close calls she had with her Mom. The others had similar experiences at their homes. Elijah suggested they go to the edge of the jungle. She was sure they could find some fruit there for Elle.

Kendall said, "Elijah, it is not safe. You know we are not supposed to go that far from the city."

Jasmine asked, "What about the wild animals?" She looked concerned as usual.

Elijah said, "If we can find something for Elle to eat, we won't have to take so much from our homes. Besides, we will have a wild animal with us."

They all laughed as they looked at Elle. She had her trunk on Elijah's shoulder. She was blowing her hair around. Elle enjoyed playing with her friends.

Tera agreed with Elijah. She said, "We should go early in the morning. Most of the animals should be asleep." So the girls spent the day making plans for the morning trip. They decided who would bring the different supplies. They agreed to meet at Elijah's house after their parents had left for work.

CHAPTER 5:
TRIP TO THE JUNGLE

Elijah was very excited about their trip to the jungle. She was ready for the adventure. As soon as the door closed behind her Mom, she raced around the house getting the supplies. She hurried to the back yard. Every morning she was still excited to see Elle had stayed. She had even got used to the morning trumpet greeting. Her friends soon arrived.

Jasmine voiced her concern about the wild animals again. Elijah assured her it would be okay. The four girls and their new elephant friend headed to the river. They would follow it to the edge of the jungle. When the girls reached the river, they decided to take a break. They had to wait on Elle to play in the water, anyway. It seems that she couldn't pass up a chance to play.

They finally persuaded the elephant out of the river so they could continue the day's adventure. Although the girls talked continuously, they were still aware of their surroundings. They knew of the possible dangers they could encounter along the way.

Jasmine suddenly shouted, "STOP!" They all froze in place, even Elle. The three girls looked at Jasmine's serious expression. Then they looked down at what she was staring at. It was a snake.

Tera softly instructed the others to slowly back up. After they had each taken five steps backwards, she said, "This should be a safe distance. We should be able to walk around it now." The others followed her without saying a word. They trusted Tera to know about these things. She had been to the jungle several times before with her Dad. This was the first time for her to go without him.

The rest of the way to the jungle was uneventful. The friends were glad. When they reached the shade of the large trees, they decided to sit down and have lunch. They didn't talk today while they ate. They were tired and they were concerned about the danger they could encounter.

CHAPTER 6:
THE JUNGLE

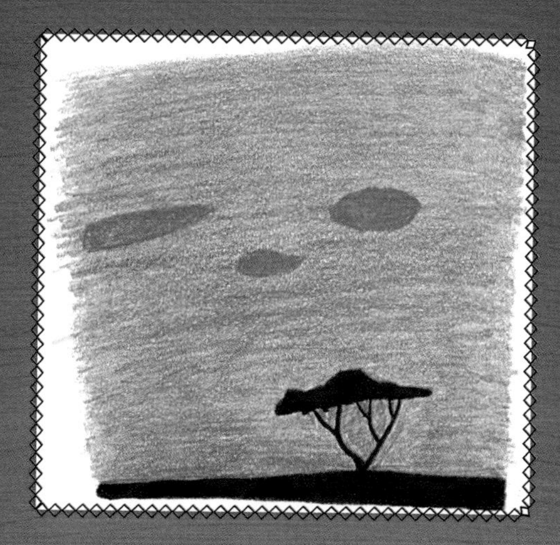

As soon as the girls finished eating, they started unpacking their supplies. They had a knife for cutting the fruit. They had several bags to haul the fruit in. It was decided that Elijah would sit on Jasmine's shoulders. She would try to reach the fruit, cut it, and hand it down to the other two. This worked for the low branches. However, they did not collect very much fruit.

The girls decided to sit down and think of a new plan. After a few minutes, Elijah suggested, "Maybe I could climb the tree." The others pointed out that even the low branches were too tall to reach. Then, Kendall had an idea. She said, "What about my walking stick? We could use it to knock down the fruit." The others agreed it was worth a try.

Since Kendall was the tallest, she tried first. She could reach a few of them. Then Elijah climbed on Jasmine's shoulders again. She was able to knock a few more down. The girls decided they had enough for this trip. They packed their supplies and started home.

The walk back to town took twice as long as the walk to the jungle. The girls and Elle had to stop several times to rest. It was dusk when the girls arrived at Elijah's house. The girls helped Elijah put the bags of fruit under the house. Then they hurried home. Elijah gave Elle some fruit for the night and hurried into the house.

Elijah was closing the back door as her Mom was opening the front. Her Mom was too tired from work to realize Elijah was just walking in the house. She asked Elijah to wash up and help her with dinner. Elijah was relieved she was not in trouble. She hoped her friends were as lucking.

CHAPTER 7:
THE GREAT IDEA

The next morning, the girls all met at Elijah's house. She told her friends how close she came to getting caught. Tera said, "I was lucky, too. My Dad came home really late. He didn't have a clue."

Jasmine said, "My Dad had his nose buried in a book. He didn't even notice I came in the house. I even slammed the door on my way in. I was lucky."

It was Kendall's turn. She didn't look happy. She said, "My parents were both home already. They asked me where I had been and why I was late. I told them I was at Elijah's house helping her with chores. Well, it was true, mostly. You know I'm not good at lying, especially to my parents. They told me it better not happen again"

The girls were still tired from the trip to the jungle. They decided to skip going to the playground today. They headed for the river. Elle was happy to get to the water. It was becoming a very hot day already. The girls sat on the river bank. They talked and watched Elle play.

Elijah told her friends, "I wish I could find a way to help my Mom. She works so hard and so many hours. I'm not old enough to get a job. Besides, I doubt my Mom would let me."

The other girls understood. They wanted to help Elijah think of something. The girls came up with several ideas. Each idea had a reason why it wouldn't work. The girls decided to join Elle in the water.

It was fun to play with a young elephant in the river. Elle was still young. She had grown a lot in size since the first day the girls met her. Elle liked to spray the girls with water from her trunk. Today she did something new. Elijah was standing in front of her and talking to her. Elle wrapped her trunk around Elijah's waist. She picked her up and tossed her into the water. The three friends stood and stared. They didn't know what to think. Elijah popped up out of the water. She started laughing. She exclaimed, "That was fun!"

Elijah walked back to Elle. She said to Elle, "Do that again." It seemed like the elephant understood. She picked Elijah up and tossed her into the water again. The girls stood, still amazed. After watching Elijah do it several more times, the others decided to try it, too. Elle did the same to them. Elle seemed to enjoy it as much as the girls.

After a while, they were tired and hungry. They decided to go back to town to eat lunch. They sat in Elijah's backyard to eat. Elle laid down to rest, too. Tera said to Elijah, "Why don't you try to teach her some tricks?" She was pointing at Elle.

Elijah replied, "Like what?" She looked at Tera with a curious expression.

"Well," Tera said and then paused. "Like the stuff elephants do at a carnival. I remember seeing an elephant do tricks at a carnival my Dad took me to when I was little."

"I have a better idea." Jasmine said proudly. "Elijah, you should train Elle to help with chores and jobs. Maybe you could get some of the business men to pay you. You said you wanted to help your Mom. Elle could learn to carry stuff and move stuff. You could have your own business."

No one said a word for several minutes. They were all considering the idea. Then Elijah finally broke the silence. She said, "That is a great idea Jasmine. I think it just might work. Mom would have to let me keep Elle if she is helping us."

Kendall added, "And we won't have to make trips to the jungle for elephant food. We won't have to keep the secret from our parents anymore." They all liked that thought.

Elijah pointed out, "We can't tell anyone yet. We have to train her first. I'm sure it won't take long. Elle is very smart." They talked the rest of the afternoon about what Elle would need to learn to be able to work.

CHAPTER 8:
LEARNING NEW TRICKS

Elijah and her friends spent the next few weeks working with Elle. They worked with her in the mornings until lunch. Afternoons were spent playing in the river. They were on school break after all.

Elijah taught Elle several commands. She taught her to lift the item she was pointing to when she said, "Lift Elle." She taught her to carry the item when she moved and said, "Carry Elle." She taught her to set the item down when she pointed and said, " Down Elle."

They worked with her using different items they could find. Elle learned the commands quickly. She really enjoyed the attention she was receiving. She especially liked the girls clapping if she did something right.

Tera suggested, "Elijah you should teach her to give rides. She could taxi people around town." Elijah shook her head yes as she started to think of how she would teach this new trick to Elle.

"I don't know if that is a good idea," Kendall remarked. "Someone could get hurt."

Elijah sighed. She looked at Elle and then at Kendall. "Do you really think Elle would hurt someone?" she asked.

"No. I guess not." Kendall replied.

So, with the help of her friends, Elijah taught Elle how to taxi people. She first taught her to lie down. Then she had to be still while the person climbed on her back and sat behind her head. Then she taught her to rise and walk with someone on her back. Next, Elijah taught the elephant how to lie down and let the person get off her back. It took two weeks for Elle to learn all of the steps to be a taxi.

Elle had grown a lot during this training time. She was now large enough to carry two of the girls on her back at a time. Elle was also eating a lot more now. The girls were having to make more trips to the jungle. They had been lucking to not run into danger. They knew their luck might run out. Elijah decided it was time for Elle to meet the people in the neighborhood.

CHAPTER 9:
ELLE'S FIRST JOB

Elijah thought about how she should introduce Elle. How does a person introduce an elephant to a neighborhood, to adults. She thought about it for a long time before she finally drifted off to sleep. That night, Elijah had several weird dreams.

She woke up tired, but she had an idea. She shared it with her friends when they arrived that morning. She said, "I think I should go visit some businesses without Elle. I will tell them I have a friend who can do a job for them. If they agree, I will come back and get Elle. You will have to stay with her so she doesn't follow me."

The girls agreed this was a good idea. Once the people met Elle, they would have to love her as much as they did. Kendall decided to go with Elijah to help her negotiate. Elijah appreciated Kendall's help. She knew Kendall was really good with words and adults. Jasmine and Tera would stay and watch Elle.

Soon, Elijah and Kendall returned. The man at the lumberyard had some inventory that needed to be unloaded from a truck. The truck was behind the warehouse building by the backdoor. It was a perfect job. Hopefully, no one would notice Elle until she was done with the job. By then, she would prove how useful she was.

The girls headed down the alley to the lumberyard. Before they arrived, Jasmine suggested she go ahead. She would distract the workers to make sure they stayed out of view until the job was complete. Jasmine was good at distractions. They agreed. Tera and Kendall were on watch while Elijah and Elle worked.

The job was done by noon. It was now time to get paid and introduce Elle to the man who owned the lumberyard. Elijah was very nervous. This was an unusual emotion for her. She was worried about whether he would accept Elle.

Elijah left Elle with Kendall and Tera. She found Jasmine. Then she found the man who had agreed to the job. He was surprised they were done already. He said he wanted to see for himself before he paid her.

Elijah agreed. She said, "I want you to meet my friend, Elle, who did all of this hard work. Before you do, I want to tell you about her." As they walked toward the backdoor, Elijah tried to describe Elle as best she could without saying the word elephant. The man had a puzzled look on his face as he walked outside.

When he saw Elle, he stopped. Then he asked, "Is that an elephant?" Before anyone could reply, he started walking toward her. Then he muttered, "Well of course it is."

The girls were happy to see he was not afraid of the elephant. He walked right up to her. Elle stuck out her trunk and shook his hand. The man stood amazed. Then he turned to Elijah. He asked, "Is this your elephant?"

Elijah thought for a minute. She wasn't quite sure what to say. Then she said, "She is part of my family." She thought it was best to not tell him too much.

Then he asked, "Where did she come from?"

Kendall replied, "She found us and she was alone."

The man looked at each of the girls. Then he looked at Elle. He turned to Elijah and reached into his pocket. He said, "Here is the money I owe you for a job well done. Come back next week with her and I will have another job."

They said in unison, "Thank you sir. We will!" He returned to the warehouse.

CHAPTER 10:
MORE WORK FOR ELLE

The girls were excited their first job was a success. They went back to Elijah's house for lunch. Elle was ready to rest. Elijah decided to have Elle do one more job before she told her Mom. So, after lunch, Elijah and Kendall went back to the businesses. Jasmine and Tera stayed with Elle.

Several of the business owners did not believe the girls. They were told to leave and quit bothering people who were working. Finally, they went to the edge of town. A new building was being built by an out-of-town company. Maybe they would have a job for Elle.

After talking to several men, they finally found the foreman. He was the man who made the decisions. Elijah asked him if he had any hauling or moving work.

He looked at Kendall and then at Elijah. He replied with a smile, "Nothing the two of you could handle."

Kendall said, "Not us. We have a friend who is very strong but doesn't talk. If you have a job for our friend, we will bring our friend back here." She was very careful with the words she used. She didn't want him to figure out she was talking about an elephant.

He thought for a minute. He decided he would give this person a chance since one of his workers was sick. He didn't want to get any further behind on the building. He said to the girls, "Bring your friend back and I will have him move some building materials."

The girls looked at each other. Elijah quickly said, "Yes sir. We will be right back. Thank you." She didn't think it was necessary to tell him Elle was a girl.

Elijah and Kendall ran all the way to Elijah's house. They were breathing so hard, they could barely tell the other two about the job. After a quick drink of water, they started walking to the building site. They decided to take the long way and go around the outskirts of the town. They thought it would be less risky and would only take a few more minutes.

When they arrived, Elle decided to give a loud trumpet hello to the other workers. They hadn't noticed her until then. The workers looked up and saw the elephant. They dropped whatever was in their hands and ran. Most of them were not from that area and had not seen an elephant up close.

The girls yelled, "It's okay! She's friendly."

The workers were hiding behind the trucks now. Elijah told her friends to stay with Elle. She walked over to the workers. She looked for the foreman. She told him, "Her name is Elle and she is our friend. She won't hurt you I promise. She is the friend I told you about. She is here to work. She is stronger than all of your men put together." She said this as she looked at the men hiding behind the truck.

The foreman looked at Elle and then at Elijah. Scratching his head he said, "I don't know about this."

Elijah had an idea. She said, "How about if you let her work for you this afternoon. If you think she has done a good job, then you will pay us. If you aren't happy, then we will leave and it won't cost you anything."

After some thought and talking to his workers, he agreed. Elijah was so happy, she hugged him. She said, "Thank you! Thank you! You won't be sorry. This was out of character for her.

Elle and the girls worked hard that afternoon. The foreman kept a close eye on them. He was still very skeptical. By the end of the work day, though, he was impressed. Elle had done the work of three of his men. She didn't complain and she didn't take breaks. She was a good worker. She had done a good job.

He walked over to the girls and the elephant. He was nervous about being so close to her. Elle, as usual, reached out with her trunk and shook his hand. He was surprised at first. Then he smiled. He said, "Nice to meet you, too." They all laughed.

The foreman paid Elijah. He said he would have more work for her tomorrow afternoon. Elijah agreed to have Elle there after lunch. The girls walked to Elijah's house.

Tera asked Elijah if she had figured out how to tell her Mom. Elijah nodded her head yes. She said, "I think I will show her the money we earned first. Then I will explain how. Hopefully, she will be so happy about the money, she won't be mad at me." Her friends wished her good luck as they headed to their homes.

CHAPTER 11:
TELLING ELIJAH□S MOM

Elijah settled Elle in for the night. Elijah was excited and nervous about telling her Mom. She really didn't know how her Mom would react. She was proud she had found a way to help her Mom. She hoped her Mom would feel the same way.

Elijah had her chores done when her Mom arrived home from work. Her Mom was tired but seemed to be in a good mood. Elijah was hopeful. She helped her Mom prepare dinner. She decided to wait until after dinner to tell her Mom.

After clearing the table, Elijah sat down with her Mom. She took her Mom's hand and said, "Mom, I love you." Her Mom looked at her with a smile. Then Elijah said, "Mom, I have something to give you." Elijah took the money out of her pocket and gave all of it to her Mom.

Her Mom was confused. She asked Elijah, "Where did you get this?" At first, Elijah just smiled. She was searching for what to say next.

Elijah finally said, "Mom, I have a big surprise to tell you about. First, let me tell you the whole story. Please let me tell you everything before you say anything and please don't be mad." Her Mom agreed.

Elijah started from the beginning. She told her about finding the elephant at the playground. Then about taking care of her. She even told her about the trips to the edge of the jungle. She told her about training Elle. Last, she told her about the money she and Elle had earned from working that day. She also told her about the agreement for more work.

Her Mom didn't say anything at first. She was thinking about all that Elijah had told her. She also thought about how much they could use the extra money. Then she spoke. She said, "Elijah, I don't know what to say. Maybe I should meet this elephant first."

Elijah was excited. Her Mom wasn't yelling and she wanted to meet Elle. This was very hopeful. Her Mom followed her out the back door. Thankfully, Elle was lying down. She didn't look as big as when she stood. Her Mom hesitated. Then she walked right up to the elephant. Elijah introduced them. Elle stuck out her trunk and shook her hand.

Elijah's Mom turned to her and said with a smile, "At least she has good manners." Then she said, "Elijah, we are going to have to talk about this." That is just what they did. They sat down in front of Elle and talked.

CHAPTER 12:
CAN ELLE STAY MOM, PLEASE?

Elijah and her Mom talked until it was past bedtime. Elijah told her Mom some of the adventures they had with Elle. She told her about how the big, tough, construction workers were scared when they saw Elle for the first time.

Then Elijah's Mom laid down some rules. If Elijah and Elle followed the rules, Elle could stay. If not, they would have to find a new home for her. They both knew Elle could not return to the wild herds now. She would not know how to take care of herself and they would probably not accept her. She would also be vulnerable to the hunters. Elijah agreed to follow the rules. Then her Mom sent her to bed. It had been a long day for all three of them.

Elijah's friends arrived early the next morning. They couldn't wait to hear what Elijah's Mom had said. Elijah decided to tease her friends. She looked very sad when she walked out to the back yard. She didn't say a word as she plopped onto the ground. Then she made a big sigh.

Her three friends looked sad, too. Then Tera finally spoke. She said, "So, your Mom said no."

Elijah looked at her friends. Then she replied, "Well, sort of. She said we couldn't go to the jungle anymore." Her friends looked at her confused. Then Elijah said with a smile, "She said Elle could stay if we follow the rules!" The girls jumped up and started dancing around. They were as excited as they were when they found Elle.

When the girls tired, they sat down by Elle. Elijah explained the rules her Mom had said. The girls listened carefully. They wanted to help Elijah keep Elle. The girls agreed the rules were fair. They were glad they would not have to go to the jungle anymore.

Elle worked various jobs around town that summer. The neighbors became accustomed to seeing Elle walk through their neighborhood. As they met her, they all became friends to Elle. She turned out to be very helpful. She even helped some of the elders by giving them a taxi ride. The other children in town had fun playing with Elle. They especially liked being sprayed with water at the river.

Elle became a member of the neighborhood. Elijah lay in bed one night thinking about all the events that summer. She thought to herself, "This has been a great summer!"

Edwards Brothers, Inc.
Thorofare, NJ USA
October 20, 2011